IN A DARK, DARK WOOD

DARK WOOD

David A. Carter

SIMON & SCHUSTER BOOKS FOR YOUNG READERS

Published by Simon & Schuster

New York • London • Toronto • Sydney • Tokyo • Singapore

In a dark, dark wood,

there was a dark, dark house.

And in that dark, dark house,

there was a dark, dark room.

And in that dark, dark room,

there was a dark, dark cupboard.

And in that dark, dark cupboard,

there was a dark, dark shelf.

And on that dark, dark shelf,

there was a dark, dark box.

And in that dark, dark box

there was...

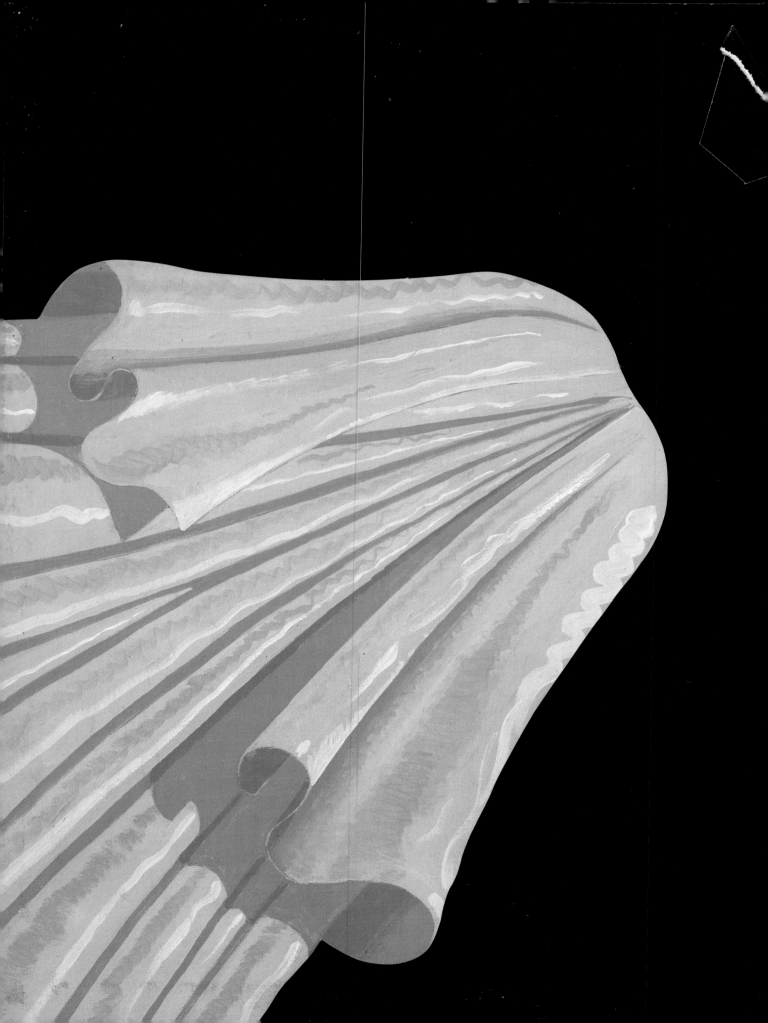